E BRO
3525000077367
89ye
Brown, Marc
Buster and the giant
pumpkin

W9-BPL-321

7/05

Buster and the Giant Pumpkin

by Marc Brown

 LITTLE, BROWN AND COMPANY

New York ~ Boston

Copyright © 2005 by Marc Brown. All rights reserved.

Little, Brown and Company, Time Warner Book Group
1271 Avenue of the Americas, New York, NY 10020 • www.lb-kids.com
First Edition
Library of Congress Cataloging-in-Publication Data
Brown, Marc Tolon.
Buster and the giant pumpkin / Marc Brown.—1st ed.   p. cm.—(Postcards from Buster)
Summary: Buster sends postcards to his friends back home when he goes to Oregon and
learns about pumpkins.
ISBN 0-316-15887-9 (hc)/ISBN 0-316-00111-2 (pb)
[1. Pumpkins--Fiction. 2. Rabbits—Fiction. 3. Postcards—Fiction. 4. Seattle (Wash.)—Fiction.] I. Title. II.
Series: Brown, Marc Tolon. Postcards from Buster. PZ7.B81618Biy 2005 [E]—dc22   2004016163

Printed in the United States of America • 10 9 8 7 6 5 4 3 2 1

SHOREWOOD PUBLIC LIBRARY

Page 20 pumpkin pie: © Royalty Free/Corbis. All other photos, except page 25 bottom, from Postcards from Buster courtesy
of WGBH Boston, and Cinar Productions, Inc., in association with Marc Brown Studios.

Do you know what these words MEAN?

champion: a person or thing that is the winner of a contest or game

coach: a large closed carriage, usually pulled by horses

contest: a game, race, or competition that people try to win

jug: a round container that usually holds liquids

measure: to find out the size, weight, or amount of something

prepared: ready

pound: one pound = 16 ounces. 1,000 pounds is about how much a large cow weighs

pumpkin: a large orange fruit with a hard rind and soft insides. Pumpkins grow on vines.

Oregon

- The world's largest pumpkin came from Oregon.

- Oregon is the only state with an official state nut: the hazelnut.

- Oregon has the world's shortest river. It is only 120 feet long. It connects Devil's Lake to the nearby Pacific Ocean.

- Oregon has the deepest lake in the U.S. It's called Crater Lake and was formed by an ancient volcano.

"That's a really big suitcase," said Arthur.

"Well, I'm going to Oregon," said Buster.

"Everything is big there. So I need to be prepared."

In Oregon, Buster met a farmer.
His name was Steve.

Steve had a son named Scotty.

They grew really big vegetables.

Alan "The Brain" Pow...

22 Oak Street

Elwood Ci...

"Last spring we planted the seed in a milk jug," said Scotty.

"But now it's growing outside."

Dear Binky,
Pumpkins grow fast here.
They can gain fifteen
pounds a day.
Even _you_ can't eat
that much.

Buster

Binky Barnes
10 Pine Tree Road
Elwood

Steve and Scotty's pumpkin
had grown big over the summer.

Buster watched them measure it.

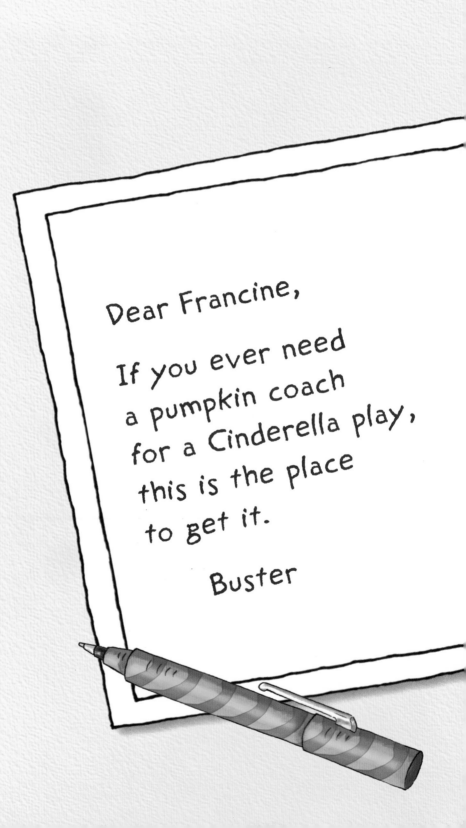

Francine Frensky
Maple Drive
Elwo...

Steve and Scotty
got the pumpkin ready to move.

Then they put it carefully
in the truck.

They planned to enter it
in a contest.

Mom Baxter
15 Willow Wa
Elwood City

Buster saw lots of big pumpkins.

The contest was about to start.

Muffy Crosswire
432 Valley View
Elwood City

The pumpkins were weighed,
one at a time.

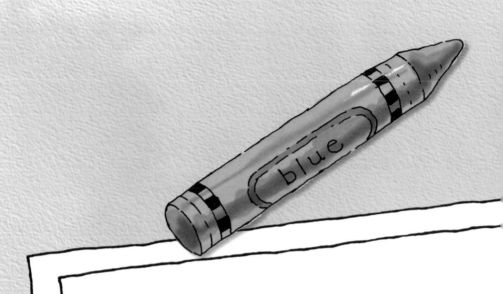

Dear Arthur,

I think every pumpkin in this contest weighs more than 1,000 pounds.

I was surprised the scale didn't break.

Buster

Arthur Read
100 Main Street
Elwood City

Scotty's pumpkin was the biggest one of all.

"1,414.5 pounds!" said Buster.

It was a new world record!

Dear Scotty,

You are a champion
pumpkin grower.

And I am a champion
pumpkin pie eater.

We make a good team!

Buster